Iliana the Iguana

Iliana Fotopoulos

Cover and
Illustrations:

Andrea hiotis

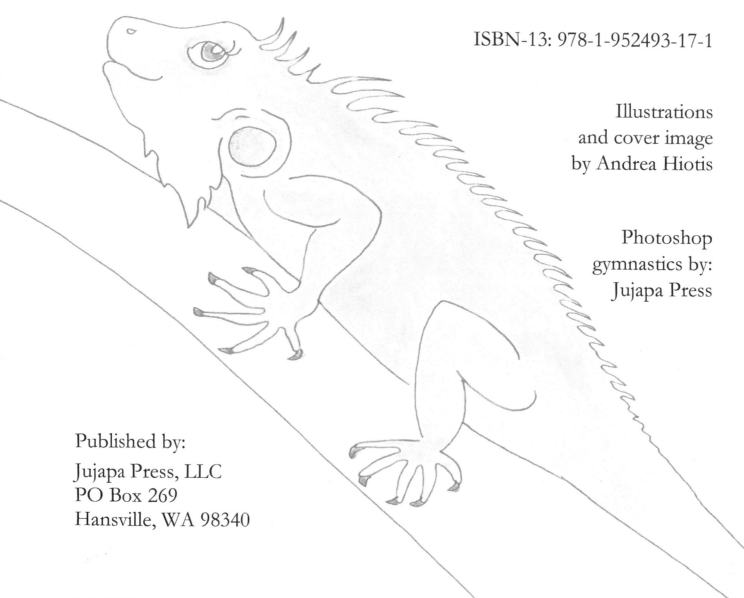

ISBN-13: 978-1-952493-17-1

Illustrations
and cover image
by Andrea Hiotis

Photoshop
gymnastics by:
Jujapa Press

Published by:
Jujapa Press, LLC
PO Box 269
Hansville, WA 98340

NOTE: The views, preferences and opinions expressed by the author in these pages belong solely to the author and do not necessarily reflect the views, preferences and opinions of Jujapa Press, LLC, or anyone other than the authors.

ACKNOWLEDGEMENTS

Iliana would like to thank her wonderful illustrator, Andrea Hoitis for her talent and creativity.

———

Andrea would like to thank Rita and Iliana Fotopoulos for making this book happen.

It's a perfect life
in the mango tree
for the Iguanas,
but...

...Iliana the Iguana
seems restless.

She runs to the
next door oak tree.

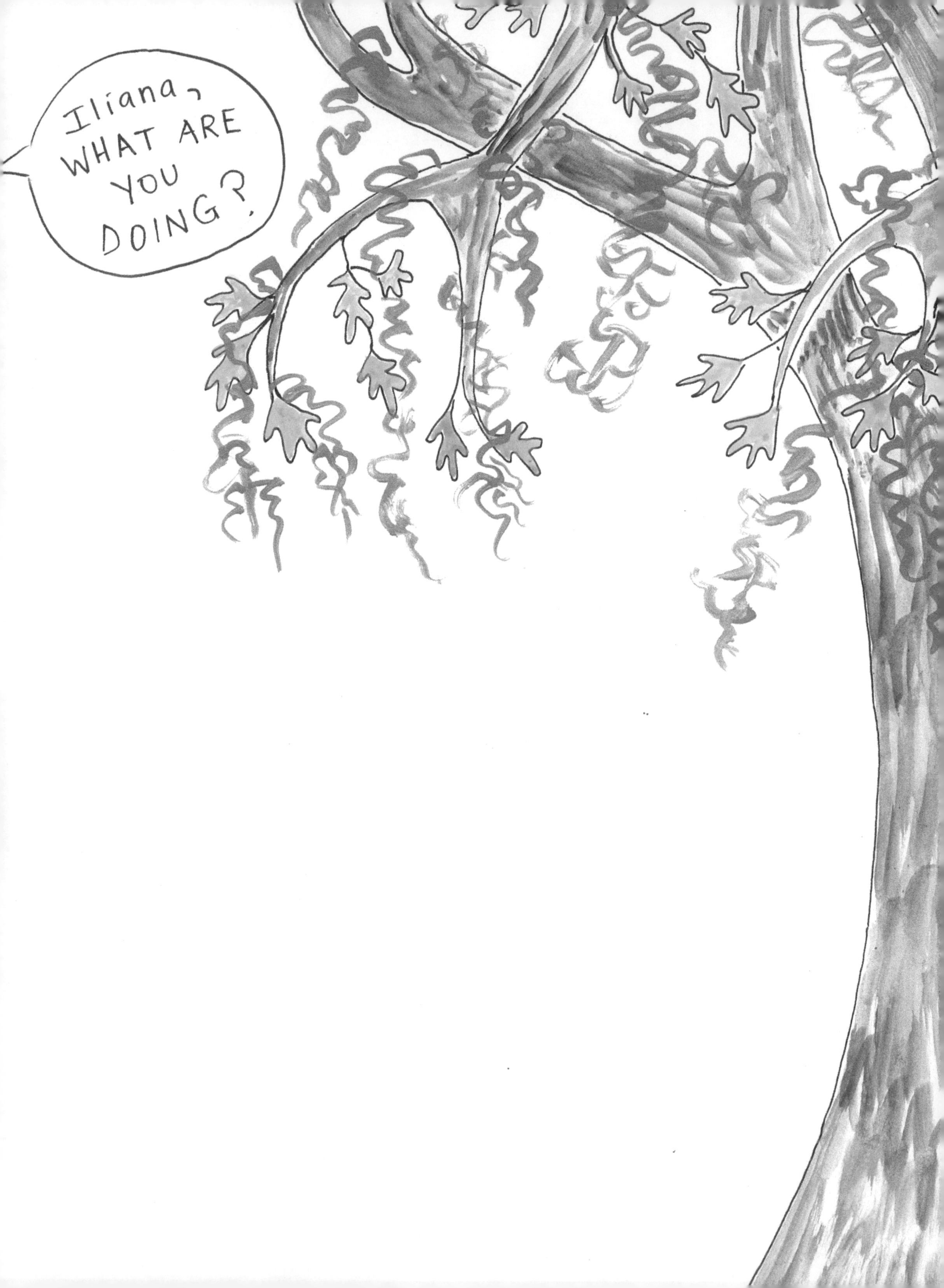
Iliana, WHAT ARE YOU DOING?

She pulls and weaves a
bed of Spanish moss...

...from the oak tree to under the mango tree.

The other iguanas
think she's
crazy
but Iliana

knits a beret
for herself...

...and a scarf.

She also knits
four nice mittens
for herself.

Suddently
a cold front moves
in and the iguanas are freezing.

They land into the
bed of moss and
cover up.

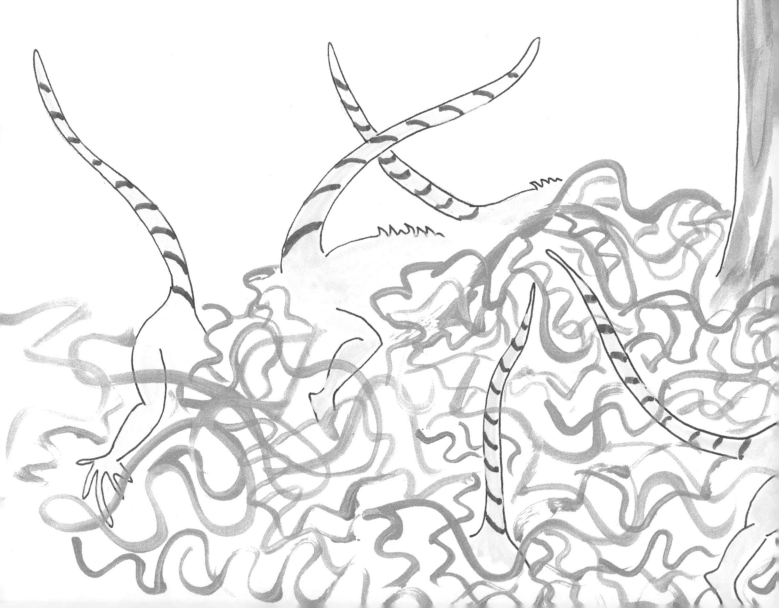

Thank you, Iliana!
Iliana is Incredible!
Iliana is Ingenious!
Iliana is Imaginative!
Iliana is Intelligent!
We love you, Iliana!

CPSIA information can be obtained
at www.ICGtesting.com
Printed in the USA
JSHW060944300622
27676JS00004B/47

9 781952 493171